Urban Legends
of The South

by Deborah Lamb

PAGE PUBLISHING, INC.
Conneaut Lake, PA

First originally published by Page Publishing 2020

ISBN 978-1-68409-063-1 (pbk)
ISBN 978-1-66243-348-1 (hc)
ISBN 978-1-68409-064-8 (digital)

Printed in the United States of America

I dedicate this book to Kebee, my children,
my grand children,
and my great grand children.

THE WATCHFUL SOULS OF SLOSS FURNACES

For the past 130 years, Sloss Furnaces has been under the watchful eye of those from years past.

In the industrial section of Birmingham, Alabama, on fifty acres of land sits Sloss Furnaces, once one of the largest producers of pig iron in the world. Sloss Furnaces, in her prime, produced iron for nearly ninety years, placing Birmingham, Alabama, on the map. Today, Sloss Furnaces is a National Historic Landmark.

It was after the Civil War in 1881 when James W. Sloss constructed Sloss Furnaces on land that was donated by the Elyton Land Company. Harry Hargreaves, an engineer born in Europe, was placed in charge of the construction of Sloss Furnaces.

Thomas Whitwell, a British inventor, was hired by Harry Hargreaves to design the stoves for Sloss. These stoves were what supplied the hot-air blast for the new furnaces. Each of these stoves was sixty feet high and eighteen feet in diameter. The Whitwell stoves that were designed for Sloss were the first of this type built in Birmingham and were comparable to the equipment that was used in the North.

In April of 1882, Sloss went into blast operation. After the first year of production, Sloss produced and sold twenty-four thousand tons of iron. When the Louisville Exposition was held in 1883, Sloss won a bronze medal for best pig iron. In 1886, James W. Sloss retired and sold the company to a group of investors. Sloss began going through a rapid expansion and reorganized in 1899 as Sloss-Sheffield Steel and Iron. As additional furnaces and extensive mineral lands were being purchased, Sloss-Sheffield was rapidly becoming the second largest pig iron merchant in the Birmingham district and among the largest in the world. It was at this point, Sloss owned seven blast furnaces, 1500 beehive coke ovens, land that was rich in coal and ore, five Jefferson County Coal Mines, red and brown ore mines, as well as quarries. By the time World War I began, Sloss-Sheffield was one of the largest pig iron producers in the world.

As World War II was beginning in the late 1930s, it opened the door for an expanded market of iron and steel which in turn created jobs for the people of Birmingham. By 1941, as the United States entered into World War II, it was estimated that nearly one-half of the workforce worked in iron, steel, and mining industries. It was estimated that of those workers, more than two-thirds were African American.

By the late nineteenth century, Birmingham's population began to rise fast. As a result, Sloss Furnaces as well as other industries began building low-cost housing. The forty-eight homes that were constructed, sat next to the site of Sloss Furnaces. "The Quarters," what these homes were referred to, were built in a shotgun style, and were built especially for the black workers and their families. Along with the houses, Sloss also set up a commissary and a doctor's office.

Also nearby, the children had access to Thomas Elementary School. This proved to be excellent for these children since educational opportunities were so poor in the 1930s and 1940s. By doing this for their employees, they felt this would cut down on absenteeism, and give their employees a sense of being part of a family, as well as a sense of security.

By the late 1950s, "The Sloss Quarters" were dismantled. This was done due to the high cost of maintenance and repairs in order to keep these houses up to quality living standards. With higher wages coming into play and much improved transportation, this helped those that lived in "Sloss Quarters" to find housing elsewhere.

Technological changes began to hit Birmingham's industrial economy in the 1960s and 1970s. As ductile and plastic pipe were on the rise, as well as increasing reliance of scrap iron, the merchant pig iron industry was declining. As stricter pollution guidelines and foreign imports were increasing, as well as mismanagement of the industry, a rapid decline began in the American Steel and Iron industry which included Sloss Furnaces. It was in 1969, when Jim Walter Corporation purchased Sloss Furnaces from U.S. Pipe and Foundry. Within two years, Sloss Furnaces, the oldest running blast furnace in Birmingham, Alabama, shut their doors.

In 1981, Sloss Furnaces was named as a National Historic Landmark and reopened in September of 1983, as a museum in the city of Birmingham. Today, Sloss Furnaces Museum consists of two 400-ton blast furnaces and approximately forty other buildings. Although there are no remains of the original Sloss complex, there is one building still standing that dates back to 1902. In this building, it houses the eight steam-driven "blowing-engines" that once provided the air for combustion in the furnaces. These engines, themselves, date back to 1900–1902 and are unique, as well as important because they helped in powering America's Industrial Revolution.

Working conditions at Sloss Furnaces in the 19th Century was extremely hard as well as dangerous. Because of this, many deaths occurred but there were only sixty deaths on record at the plant. Although it has been reported that there are many spirits that roam Sloss, there are two spirits that are said to be seen and heard more than any.

The first spirit that is reported to walk within Sloss is Theophilus Jowers. The story is told that Jowers loved his job so much that he called one of the furnaces his "friend." But Jowers's wife thought differently. She would express her concerns to Jowers often. She was always scared that Jowers would get hurt badly or even worse, killed. Jowers would tell his wife often to "Not worry, because the furnace is my friend. As long as there's a furnace standing in this country, I will be there." As the story continues, Jowers got up one morning and began his day just like days past. He clocked in at work and began his workday. As he was preforming his duties, he lost his balance and fell into one of his beloved furnaces.

Not long after the death of Jowers, reports began to surface of Jowers being seen walking the catwalks, as well as seeing him preforming his duties. Another report of Jowers being seen was by his son, John Jowers. It was in the year of 1927; John was driving over the viaduct with his son, Leonard. As they crossed over, he shut off the engine to the car so he and his son could watch the "Sloss as it was tapped." As they watched, John quickly grabbed Leonard's arm and pointed in the direction of the sparks. Just as Leonard looked, a man emerged from the sparks. John quickly explained to his son that, "It was way too hot for a living man to walk that close to the sparks, so it had to be the ghost of his father, Theophilus Jowers. The few people that are still alive today state "Theophilus loved the work he did at Sloss Furnaces and that is why he remains here still to this day to continue his work and to make sure everything is done."

The second spirit that is reported to walk within Sloss is James "Slag" Wormwood. The story is told that James or Slag", as his coworkers called him, was the foreman of the graveyard shift at Sloss Furnaces. There were many reports of how brutal "Slag" was to the workers he was in charge of. It was reported by some that Wormwood wanted to impress his supervisors so much that he forced his workers to undertake very dangerous duties in order to speed up production. During the summer months, temperatures within the plant would reach 120° plus which made working in the plant very hard without any breaks for these men to cool down some. The men that worked under Wormwood worked in unbearable heat, low visibility, and with a lack of sleep. These conditions combined made working the furnace a "living hell." As the story continued, Wormwood began his shift just as he did any other night. He began his night working around the furnace "Big Alice" which was the highest furnace at Sloss. It was believed that while he was working around "Big Alice," the fumes from the methane gas over took him and he fell into the furnace. It was reported that Wormwood did not work at or around "Big Alice;" therefore, many believed that some of the men that worked under him threw him into the furnace for payback because he was always such a tyrant. With only a handful of people still alive today that worked at Sloss, no one could confirm this to be really what happened.

Today, Sloss Furnaces is a museum with its rich history in playing a part in America's Industrial Revolution and is also the oldest remaining blast furnaces in Birmingham, Alabama. Sloss also has "Sloss Fright Furnace" that opens every year at Halloween starting October 6 and runs through October 31. If you ever get the chance to come to Birmingham, Alabama around Halloween, try to go through "Sloss Fright Furnace," who knows you may just run into one of the souls that have been watching over Sloss Furnaces for the last 130-plus years.

A PLAYGROUND FOR THE
CHILDREN OF THE DEAD

A playground that is said to be inhabited by children that are dead. In a beautiful little city that sits in a picturesque valley, is home to Maple Hill Cemetery, located in Huntsville, Alabama. Within the solace walls of the cemetery lays a playground. This playground is known to the residents of Huntsville as the "Dead Children's Playground."

Maple Hill Cemetery was founded in 1822 and originally had only two acres. These first two acres were sold to the City of Huntsville in September 14, 1822, from LeRoy Pope. The cemetery is located just east of the Twickenham Historic District. At present, the cemetery covers approximately 100 acres of land, making Maple Hill Cemetery, the oldest and largest cemetery in the state of Alabama. Upon entering the cemetery, it looks as though time has stood still. Maple Hill Cemetery is the final resting place for many confederate soldiers, 187 unknown confederate soldiers, and an undetermined number of union soldiers, U.S. representatives, U.S. senators, and some of Alabama's governors. It is difficult to find documented proof of burials prior to 1822, but there is evidence that the land was used for burials before the cemetery's official establishment date.

The playground within Maple Hill Cemetery is surrounded by three rock cliffs and a beautiful wooded path. By day, the cemetery has a childlike appearance and an innocent feel. But as the sun begins to go down, the playground takes on a look that most would say, is dark or even evil. It is said that the spirits of children that are dead, come to the playground to play. The legend goes on to say, that in the 1960s, Huntsville was plagued by a number of child abductions. The bodies of some of these children were found at the playground, dead. Although there are no known facts to back this story up, the residents of Huntsville stand by this story. Since the alleged abductions and killings took place, there have been reports of swings moving on their own, the voices of children calling out to each other, as well as children giggling. As pictures were being taken, it was reported that orbs would appear in them. It is believed that these orbs are that of the children that were found dead on the playground. Much of this activity happens between 10:00 p.m. and 3:00 a.m.

It is reported that when the swings begin to swing, they are in sync with one another even if they were stopped. There are also reports of dust flying up from the ground under the swing, as if someone just jumped off the swing. Some of the pictures that have been taken have a mist of light that shows up, which appears to be the height of a child. There are some reports of a man being seen sitting on one of the cliffs watching the children while they would play. Some seem to think he was the man that abducted and killed these children.

The City of Huntsville tried to take the playground over and removed the playground equipment in 2007 in order to increase the cemetery's capacity. The residents of Huntsville protested the removal of the playground and in doing so, new playground equipment was installed. After the new equipment was installed, the activity resumed just as before.

It has been said that, the children will always have a place. Once again, the playground is still there for the children to play, should they be dead or alive. Although no one is allowed in the playground at night, you can still see the lights at the playground, which is a mystery in itself. This is because there are no lights to light the playground up at night.

THE PAST FACES THAT HAUNT
ST. JAMES HOTEL TODAY

In 1881, Frank and Jessie James came to the St. James Hotel, in Selma, Alabama. Some say Jessie James never left.

In the beautiful scenic river town of Selma, Alabama, stands the picturesque St. James Hotel. Within the walls of this historic hotel, some say, lives a man by the name of Jessie James. The St. James Hotel was constructed in 1837, more than 170 years ago and overlooks the Alabama River. Originally, the hotel was named Brantly Hotel and kept this name until 1887. It was at this time the American Civil War was taking place and the union troops began to occupy the Brantly Hotel, using it for their headquarters during the Battle of Selma.

The Confederates had many arsenals and factories along the riverfront, as well as throughout the city. As the war progressed, the union troops began to burn down most of the city, but left the Brantly Hotel and a few other structures untouched on Water Street. The St. James, as well as the few other structures, left standing would form what is known today as the heart of the historic district and represents some of the "finest antebellum industrial buildings in the south," according to Historic Hotels of America.

As the war came to an end, a gentleman by the name of Benjamin S. Tower, the first African American to become a congressman, bought the St. James and rented rooms out long-term. In 1881, it is said that Frank and Jessie James rented rooms in the St James, making the hotel their headquarters.

In 1892, hard times began to fall on the little river town, causing the hotel to stop operations and close its doors, and remained closed for over 100 years. The residents of Selma pulled together in 1997, and restored the historic landmark back to its beautiful antebellum look. The doors reopened for operation, and remain open to this day.

In 1881, it is said that Frank and Jessie James moved into the St. James Hotel and never moved out. Since the reopening of the St. James in 1997, there have been many reports of an apparition of Jessie James, dressed in 1880s clothes, walking the halls around the guest rooms of 214, 314, as well as 315. He has also been reported being seen downstairs sitting at a corner table by the bar.

Jessie was also known to have had a girlfriend by the name of Lucinda. Lucinda has been described as being beautiful, very tall, with long black hair, and always smelled of the sweet scent of lavender.

Through the years, there have been many reports of the apparition of a woman, thought to be Lucinda, wandering the hotel grounds, stopping to watch the living as they would come and go. Many have said, that when her apparition appears, so does the scent of lavender. Some have said, through the years that Jessie James once owned a black dog that was his companion for many years. Many guests, while staying at the St James, have reported hearing a dog running up and down the halls. Also, guests in the hotel would often complain about a dog that would bark nonstop in the courtyard. When management would look into their complaints, no dog was ever found in the courtyard.

Throughout the years, the St. James has had its share of psychics and paranormal investigators walk the halls. While investigating the hotel, many of them would pick up more than three entities. Paranormal investigators have reported seeing groups of apparitions of people strolling around the inner courtyard, dressed in clothes dating back to the 1880s. Some investigators reported hearing glassware being banged together, and would continue until someone would say to stop. There are other reports that state, a man has been seen sitting in the drinking room on a bench.

One paranormal investigating team was in the Brantly Ballroom conducting an EVP (Electronic Voice Phenomenon) session, where one of the investigators asked a question "Is anyone here?" When the investigation was complete, they played the recording back. As they listened to the recording, they heard an answer to their question. In a very gruff and clear voice, the entity said, "Well, that's a stupid question."

The St. James Hotel has been investigated many times through the years by psychics and paranormal investigators. It is the consensus of these investigators that the St. James Hotel is in fact haunted. Selma, Alabama, is a beautiful little town to visit with all of its rich history. If you ever get the chance to pass through Selma, stop and stay a night at the St. James Hotel. Who knows? You just might get a visit from Jessie James himself.

A HAUNTING LEGEND AND GHOSTS: THE CLEVELAND HOUSE

Words spoken from a father to his young son form a bond that still echoes through the trees 153 years later.

As a child growing up in Alabama, the stories of hauntings has always been a part of the south. Each state has their ghost stories, hauntings, as well as urban legends. But, there is something about the stories in the south. They captivate and pull all those listening or reading right in, rather it be a true ghost story or an urban legend. All ghost stories or urban legends will at one time or another, leave one with an uneasy feeling. But when it involves a child, it tends to leave footprints on our heart. This is one of those stories.

In the deep south of the state of Alabama, back in the woods sits an unusual house built by Steven Cleveland. It was in 1849; Cleveland went to California to participate in the gold rush. Upon returning back to his home town, Suggsville, Alabama, he began a law practice and became active in politics. He later ran for a senate seat in the Alabama Senate, but resigned in order to enter into the military. Cleveland in 1856, took a bride by the name of Eliza Creagh, together they had two children.

In 1860, Cleveland completed the construction of his home, which was built in the unusual shape of an L, with every room of the house opening out to the large front porch as well as back porch. The Cleveland House, or better known today as the Lodge, was constructed one room deep. With each room opening to the porch, it allows for cross-ventilation. During this time in 1861, Cleveland was very active in the Civil War, and helped organize a troop of men called "The Sons of the Grays." Cleveland and his troop of men would gather in the yard of his home, and would leave for battle from there.

The legend begins when Cleveland enters the military to fight in the war. Before leaving, he chose not to wake his young son to tell him good-bye in order to avoid the emotional pain. When Walter, his son, woke from his nap, he was told his father had to leave to fight in the war. Walter was so heartbroken after he got up from his nap because his father did not wake him to tell him good-bye. When Cleveland returned home, he worked hard to make it up to his son. Cleveland sat down with Walter, his son, and made him a promise. He promised Walter, he would not leave without taking a moment to tell him good-bye. He then picked Walter up and placed him on his horse and took him for a ride. As Walter sat in the saddle, Cleveland rode up the stairs at the front of the house, around the porch, then back down the stairs at the back of the house.

As Cleveland rode Walter on his horse, he could see Walter's face light up with such joy as well as excitement, as they repeated riding up the stairs, across the porch, and back down the stairs at the rear of the house. Riding Walter on his horse became a much loved ritual before Cleveland would leave to fight in the war.

As the story continues, it is July of 1861; Cleveland has just returned home from the war and was told that his beloved son, Walter, had passed away from an unknown illness. Cleveland was so heartbroken with the tragic news of his son's passing. It was reported that Cleveland, before leaving for battle, would ride up the stairs in front, across the porch, and back down the stairs at the back of the house. As he rode, the men in his company could hear him telling his young deceased son good-bye. It was in 1883, when Steven Cleveland, a captain in the military, passed away. From the time of his young son's death in 1861, till Cleveland's death in 1883, he lived with a heart that was shattered.

Today, the Cleveland House is known as the Lodge and is privately owned. It is often used for civic groups to hold their meetings, and it is also used by hunting clubs. From the time of Cleveland's death in 1883 to the present, people have reported hearing clopping sounds, like those of a horse riding up the stairs, around the porch, and back down the stairs at the back of the house. One gentleman reported that while he and his wife, along with a cousin and his wife, stayed at the Cleveland House/ The Lodge were playing cards late one night. They were startled by a loud clopping noise. The gentleman stated it was for sure a clopping sound, like that of a horse, not a possum or a raccoon.

As they all stopped playing cards, they looked at each other. The gentleman jumped up from his chair, ran to the door and slung it open. Once out the door onto the porch, he looked in both directions, but he saw no one, nor did he see any animals. There have been many reports down through the years just like this one, but there have been a few reports that were proven to be a hoax.

You can ask anyone that was born and raised in Suggsville about the haunting at the Cleveland House, and they will tell you the clopping sounds that you hear, are those of Cleveland's horse as he rides Walter, his son, on the porch, the ride that Cleveland did not get to take before Walter's sudden death.

A Haunting Legend at Cedarhurst Mansion

A young girl dies at her home, Cedarhurst Mansion. Many have stated she will never leave the mansion she so dearly loved.

A beautiful city that sits nestled down in a valley is Huntsville, Alabama. Huntsville, too many is better known as the Rocket City. Within her mountain walls is a military community, Redstone Arsenal. Huntsville is also home to companies such as NASA and Boeing. There is something else about Huntsville that many are unaware of. This quiet little city is said to be the most haunted city in the state of Alabama. One of the many haunting legends in Huntsville would be that of the haunting of Sally Carter at the Cedarhurst Mansion.

Cedarhurst Mansion was built in 1823 by Stephen Ewing for his wife, Mary Ewing. The mansion was a two-story brick home, with walls that were fifteen inches thick. The family plot was also located on the property of Cedarhurst. The Ewing estate had several owners throughout the years, until the early 1980s when developers purchased the property, and built townhomes. The mansion was then converted into a clubhouse called Cedarhurst Club. The Cedarhurst Club today serves as a clubhouse for the gated community of townhomes. The family plots where Mrs. Ewing, her three children and her sister, Sally Carter were laid to rest, were moved to Maple Hill Cemetery, the oldest and largest cemetery in the state of Alabama, to undisclosed locations.

As a child growing up in Huntsville, I remember being told about the ghost of Sally Carter. I remember being told that Sally Carter was killed violently while sitting on the porch of Cedarhurst.

She was hit in the head with an ax by an unknown assailant. Sally was found by her sister, Mrs. Ewing. The ax that was used to kill her was found stuck in a tree, not far from her home.

The legend goes on to say that when someone would remove the ax; it would somehow reappear in the same tree that it was found in. Another story of how Sally died said, as Sally sat in a rocker on the front porch, a man came up behind her and strangled her, breaking her pearl necklace. It is said that anytime a woman would visit the mansion, if she had a necklace on, the necklace would break with no explanation. In all reality, Sally Carter died due to a fatal illness, while visiting her sister, Mrs. Ewing. She passed away on November 28, 1837, three weeks before her 16th birthday.

Claims of seeing Sally Carter go back as far as 1919. The first person to have witnessed seeing her was a seventeen-year-old boy that was from Dothan, Alabama. When he arrived at Cedarhurst, he slept outside of Sally's bedroom. A storm began to brew as he was sleeping. The next morning he began to tell his family about the odd dream that he had the night before. He stated that a young girl, Sally, had visited him in a dream. He went on to tell his family that Sally asked him to prop up her headstone. He also told his family that he was going to go to Sally's grave. When he arrived at her grave site, he stopped. As he stood there looking, he could not believe what he was looking at. Sally's headstone had in fact fallen over from the storm the night before. After having the odd dream the night before, then seeing her headstone tipped over, the young boy left Huntsville and went back to Dothan, never to return to Huntsville again. Others that would visit Cedarhurst reported hearing footsteps going up and down the hallway. Doors that would open and close without any explanation. There were also reports of covers being snatched off of the bed and light switches that would be tripped.

From 1912 until present, Sally Carter has been sighted at the clubhouse, which was the mansion originally. She has also been sighted many times at Maple Hill Cemetery, which is her final resting place. Sally's bedroom, which is in the clubhouse and part of the original mansion, has been preserved. Upon entering her room, you step back in time and you can still feel her presence.

THE EERIE HAUNTING
SOUNDS OF DAYS PAST

The residents of this historic river town, Demopolis, Alabama state, there is a restless spirit that roams the Gaineswood Plantation.

Nestled deep in South Alabama, lays a sleepy little town, Demopolis, population approximately 7000, and covers approximately twelve square miles. Within the walls of this historic town sits a beautiful structure that has stood the test of time, Gaineswood Plantation.

In 1825, Nathan Bryan Whitfield relocated from North Carolina to Alabama's commercial river hub, Demopolis. In 1842, Whitfield purchased land from a gentleman named George Strother Gains and would soon build his plantation on this land. Property records do show that prior to 1843, a house had been built on the property that Whitfield purchased in 1821, but records do not indicate that the house was left standing or torn down.

In 1843, Whitfield began construction on what would be the largest plantation to have ever been built in Marengo County, as well as most notable due to the structure's design. The Gaineswood Plantation, because of its design, architects have labeled it as "Greek Revival Architecture."

It would take Whitfield eighteen years to complete the construction of Gaineswood Plantation, with the final touches completed in 1861. Whitfield, after the purchase of the land, and construction beginning on the mansion, he decided to name the estate "Marlmont." Soon after giving the estate its name, Whitfield learned of a treaty that was put in place between Gains, whom sold

Whitfield the land, and the chief of the Indian tribe, "Choctaw Nation."

Gaines and the tribe's chief, Pushmataha, met under one of the old oak trees, the Pushmataha Oak, where they began to discuss the placement of a treaty. This treaty that was put into place is known today as the "Choctaw Indian Removal."

With this information known, Whitfield again changed the name of the estate to "Gaineswood." He chose to change the name in order to honor George Strother Gaines. He felt the change was needed due to Gaines playing such a vital role in the history of Demopolis.

As Whitfield continued with the construction of his mansion, tragedy struck. In 1846, Whitfield's wife passed away after a long battle of an illness not known. After the death of his wife, Whitfield hired a woman by the name of Evelyn Carter to help with his children, as well as help him to maintain the running of the plantation in and outside. Whitfield continued the construction of Gaineswood when he was hit with misfortune, the death of Evelyn Carter. Just before Ms. Carter's death, she voiced her final request to Whitfield. The request she made was to take her back to Virginia to be buried in the family plot in Virginia Cemetery.

Whitfield worked to fulfill Ms. Carter's wishes, but at the time of her death, the weather was at its worse. The temperatures were dropping fast with ice forming, and snow beginning to cover the ground. Due to the frigid temperatures, he was unable to carry out Ms. Carter's wishes. Whitfield was forced to place her in a casket built from pine. He sealed her casket tight and placed her under the house until such time he could take her to her final resting place. It was at this time the legend of Evelyn Carter's ghost being seen and heard began.

The residents of Demopolis, down through the years, have told the story of the haunting sounds, and the sightings of her restless spirit as she roams the grounds of the Gaineswood Plantation, waiting to be placed in her final resting place.

Through the years, visitors have reported seeing, what they believe to be the apparition Ms. Carter in and around the grounds.

These reports led paranormal investigators to Gaineswood in order to investigate the paranormal claims. Many of the reports state, that people are hearing low whispers, soft humming, as well as singing. Some visitors reported hearing piano playing coming from within the plantation. Some have also reported hearing faint footsteps coming from many locations within the plantation. Through many investigations, the Gaineswood Plantation has been deemed as one of the most truly haunted houses in the state of Alabama.

In 1861, Nathan Whitfield passed away, leaving this magnificent plantation to his family until 1923. At that time, two more families owned and lived in the plantation until 1966, when the Alabama Historical Commission bought it. The plantation was reopened as a house museum in 1971 and remains open still today.

THE MYSTERIOUS LEGEND
OF THE BELL WITCH

The mysterious haunting of the Bell Witch in the early 1800s torturing John Bell Sr. and his family for four years, driving him to his death.

Tucked away in the upper northwest part of Tennessee, in Robertson County, sits a small picturesque town, Adams. The year was 1817 when John Bell Sr. and his family lived on a large secluded farm, located on the Red River just outside of Adams, Tennessee. The town was incorporated as Red River in 1869. It was not until 1898, Red River was renamed Adams in honor of James Reuben Adams, which owned most of the land that the town was built on. The small town of Adams was reincorporated in 1908. With its rich farmland and beautiful rolling hills, Adams was incorporated as a city. The 2000 census recorded 566 people, 203 households, and 158 families. By 2010, the population grew by sixty-seven, raising the total population to the total of 633.

Each state, as well as other countries, has at least one paranormal, ghost, or urban legend that is so profound, it is talked about for many years. Perhaps, one of the most infamous and well-documented stories comes out of the state of Tennessee, the "Bell Witch."

The Legend of the Bell Witch began in the year of 1817 when John Bell Sr. and his family occupied the large farm that was located in Robertson County, on the Red River, just outside of Adams, Tennessee. Bell was neighbors with a woman by the name of Kate Batts. It is not known the exact reason for Bell and Batts bad blood, but some stated it was a bad land deal, while others said it was a bad business deal over the purchase of slaves. Nonetheless, Bell and Batts did not get along.

As Kate Batts lay on her deathbed, she swore she would haunt John Bell Sr., his family and his entire descendant's for all the wrongs he did to her in life. "The Guidebook for Tennessee" picked up the story in 1933 by the federal government works project administration.

The first manifestation in 1817 was reported as being a strange animal that Bell saw in his cornfield. Bell shot and killed the animal and described it as having the body of a dog and the head of a rabbit. Not long after Bell killed the strange animal, began the never ending knocking, rapping, gnawing, and scratching noises outside the house. Eventually, these same noises moved into the home. Elizabeth (Betsy) Bell, youngest child of John Bell Sr., claimed she was being assaulted by an invisible force that appeared to be increasing in strength. It was reported that Betsy was slapped, pinched, bruised, and poked with pins.

Not only did the Bell family have conversations with this presence, it was reported that the guests that would visit the Bell's, this presence would have conversations with them. As time passed, this presence would identify itself as "Kate Batts." It was reported by the locals it was "Kate Batts" spirit, while others stated it was the witch "Kate Batts."

The hauntings at the Bell's farm spread throughout the state of Tennessee, making the Bell's farm famous. Before too long, the farm drew many visitors, with one of them being former General/President Andrew Jackson and his troops. After Jackson and his troops stayed one night, he was quoted as saying, "I had rather face the entire British Army than spend another night with the Bell Witch."

At one point, the Bell Witch turned her attention to John Bell Sr. According to reports; Bell would have facial seizures often with no apparent cause. On many occasions, these seizures would leave him unable to speak. Bell would often have cycles of strange and unexplained illnesses often confining him to his bed. The Bell Witch, "Kate Batts," was reported to say she was responsible for all of Bell's illnesses. Often, when Bell was sick and in his bed, he was said to be cursed at, prodded, and was never left to rest.

The last time Bell took to his bed very ill, he never recovered. There are two conflicting reports about him on the last day of his life. One states that, the next morning he was found to be senseless with a strange bottle of an unknown liquid. This statement goes on to say that Bell's breath smelled the very same as the black liquid found in the bottle next to him. The next statement goes on to say that Bell, after taking to his bed and extremely sick, he so called ingested some of the liquid from the bottle which had a very potent poison in it.

There are three facts that are the same in both versions. Fact one: The bottle found next to him had some type of liquid in it. Fact two: Bell ingested the mystery liquid found in the bottle next to him. Fact three: John Bell Sr. died December 20, 1820. After Bell died, the witnesses in the room force fed a drop of the black liquid to the Bell's cat, causing the immediate death of the cat. The witnesses in Bell's bedroom at the time of his death, reported that they could hear the Bell Witch, Kate, screaming in victory as Bell passed. Witnesses at Bell's funeral stated she could be heard laughing, cursing Bell, and singing as Bell's body was placed down in the earth.

After Bell's funeral, Kate, the Bell Witch, was not done with the survivors of John Bell Sr. It was stated that Kate turned her torment back to Betsy, Bell's youngest daughter. Kate would give Betsy verbal warnings to not marry Joshua Gardner, which was the man that she truly loved. She did, however, let Betsy marry local schoolteacher, Richard Powell.

As Kate, the Bell Witch, was leaving the Bell family, she had a few final words to say. She stated she would return to the Bell's farm in seven years. Just as she promised, Kate returned and tormented the Bell family for two more weeks.

It was in the late years of the 1800s, the Bell's secluded farm had to be torn down for the safety of the visitors local, as well as, those that traveled from all over to be a part of the mysterious Bell Witch legend. Before the Bell's farm house was torn down, there were many articles preserved. Among those articles saved were a chimney stone, an iron kettle, news articles, and photos of John Bell Sr. and his family when they lived on the farm.

The Bell's farm house was reconstructed where the original house once stood. The locals in and around Adams, Tennessee, believe Kate, the Bell Witch, still resides to this day in the cave that is on the property that John Bell Sr. owned. The Bell Witch cave, well let's just say, is for another day.

THE URBAN LEGENDS OF THE MYRTLES PLANTATION

The deep south is known for its hot lazy summer nights, church on Sunday, Sunday dinner with family and friends, and the beautiful antebellum homes rich with history. But, the deep south also has a darker side; it is home to many ghost stories, hauntings, and urban legends. Some of these legends leave one with such an unsettled feeling. In the deep south of Louisiana, sits a beautiful antebellum plantation, the Myrtles. The legend of the Myrtles Plantation is surrounded by mystery, intrigue, and death, making it one of the most haunted structures in America. It has been told through the years, approximately ten murders occurred at the Myrtles Plantation. But according to the historical records, there was only one murder that took place at the Myrtles Plantation, which was William Winter.

It was in the year of 1794 that General David Bradford was forced to leave his beautiful home he built for his wife Elizabeth and his five children in Washington County, Pennsylvania. His leaving was due to his participation in the "Whiskey Rebellion." It was rumored that President George Washington placed a price on Bradford's "Whiskey Dave" head. To protect his wife and children, Bradford left Pennsylvania, ending up near Bayou Sara, just outside of what is now called St. Francisville, Louisiana.

In 1796, Bradford purchased 600 acres of land and built an eight-room home named "Laurel Grove." Bradford lived at the plantation alone until 1799. It was then; President John Adams granted General David Bradford a full pardon for his role in the Whiskey Rebellion. In turn for the pardon, Bradford agreed to help establish a boundary line known as "Ellicott's Lane." This boundary line was between Spain and the United States. Bradford returned to Pennsylvania to bring his wife and children back to Louisiana and the plantation he built.

In 1801, Bradford returned to Pennsylvania one last time to sell the home he built for his wife, Elizabeth, and their five children. Two years passed, and Bradford still was unable to find a buyer. He finally agreed to trade the house and land for 230 barrels of flour to be delivered to his home in Bayou Sarah. Since there was a shortage of flour in New Orleans, Bradford thought he could sell the barrels to make up for the loss of money for his house in Pennsylvania. Sadly, Bradford never received the flour, despite him trying repeatedly to collect until his death in 1817.

On occasion, Bradford would take in people that wanted to study law. One of those students was Clark Woodrooff. At age nineteen, Woodrooff's dream was not farming as was his father's. So he left Connecticut and followed the Mississippi River. He ended up in Bayou Sarah, Louisiana, in 1810. After settling in, Woodrooff opened an academy in September of 1811. His curriculum for the academy was English, grammar, astronomy, geography, elocution, and composition. Before Woodrooff knew, the Academy's doors were closed. Woodrooff joined Colonel Hides regiment to fight alongside of Andrew Jackson at the Battle of New Orleans.

Woodrooff returned to Bayou Sarah after the war, and began his studies for his law degree under Bradford. It was during this time that Woodrooff met Sarah Mathlida, his professor's daughter, and fell in love with her. After Woodrooff earned his law degree, he married Sarah Mathlida in November 19, 1817. He then moved into "Laurel Grove" with his new bride. Together, they had three children.

Tragedy struck in 1817, when Bradford, Woodrooff's father-in-law passed away. Woodrooff and his family remained at the plantation so he could manage it for his mother-in-law, Elizabeth. While taking care of the plantation, Woodrooff expanded, planting 650 acres of indigo and cotton. A few years go by, when tragedy hits the Woodrooff/Bradford family again. It was July 21, 1823, Sarah Mathlida, Woodrooff's wife, and Elizabeth Bradford's daughter, passed away after contracting yellow fever. Woodrooff was devastated with the passing of his wife, but continued to manage "Laurel Grove" and take care of his mother-in-law, Elizabeth, as well as his three children. Woodrooff was hit hard again. On July 15, 1824, he lost his only son to yellow fever. Woodrooff, still grieving from the loss of his wife, and then his son, was extremely difficult for him. Tragedy hit Woodrooff once again two months later. In September, Woodrooff loses another child, a daughter, to the dreaded disease, yellow fever.

By this time, Woodrooff was a broken man and filled with grief, he somehow finds a way to pull himself up. Woodrooff purchased the plantation, "Laurel Grove" from his mother-in-law, Elizabeth. He remained on the plantation along with Elizabeth, and his only remaining child, Octavia. In 1830, Elizabeth Bradford passed away, so Woodrooff decided to leave the plantation and move to New Orleans, leaving a caretaker in charge of Laurel Grove Plantation. At this point, Woodrooff decided to change the spelling of his last name, from Woodrooff to Woodruff and began to practice law. Once he was settled, he was appointed to a judge's position in District D in Covington, Louisiana.

January 1, 1834, Woodruff decided to sell Laurel Grove Plantation to Ruffin Grey Stirling. After he sold the plantation, Woodruff left his position as a Judge in 1835, and was elected to the President of Public Works for the city of New Orleans. His only remaining child, Octavia, went to finishing school in Connecticut. In 1836, Octavia returned home and lived with Woodruff. Two years later, in 1838, Octavia married a very wealthy man, Colonel Lorenzo Augustus Besancon. After the couple married, they moved to Oaklawn, the Besancon's family plantation.

In 1840, Governor Isaac Johnson appointed Woodruff to a new office of auditor of public works. Woodruff remained in this position for one term. At age sixty, Woodruff retired and moved to Oaklawn Plantation to live with his daughter, Octavia and his son-in-law. He remained there until his death, November 25, 1851.

Woodruff was buried in the Girod Street Cemetery. There is a small tidbit of information about the cemetery Woodruff was buried in. For many years, the cemetery became neglected, and overgrown, and eventually abandoned. In the 1960s, the city decided to renovate the area where the cemetery was located. Notices were sent to the families of those buried in the cemetery. Those graves that no one claimed were placed in drums and buried in mass graves. Woodruff was one of those graves that no one claimed. This cemetery was located where the Superdome is today.

The family that bought Laurel Grove in 1834 was very wealthy, owning plantations on both sides of the Mississippi. Stirling not only bought Laurel Grove, he also purchased all of the land, buildings, and all of the slaves. Stirling began renovations on the plantation. He added a broad central hallway, and an entire southern section. Stirling had all four walls removed and repositioned them to create four large rooms, two parlors for men, and two parlors for ladies. The Stirlings made several trips to Europe to purchase fine furnishings. He built a 107 foot long gallery in the front of the plantation, and extended the original roof to cover the new edition. To complete all of the renovations, Stirling changed the name of Laurel Grove to Myrtles Plantation. He was only to enjoy the plantation he newly renovated for four more years. In 1854, Ruffin Stirling passed away from TB or Tuberculosis. In those days, it was referred to as consumption.

Mary Cobb, Stirling's widow, was left all of his holding, and ran all of them by herself. Stirling had a term of endearment that he called her, which was a "remarkable woman." Ruffin and Mary both were successful when it came to finances, but were not that lucky when it came to their family. The couple has nine children, but tragically lost five of them. One of their daughters, Sarah Mulford, married William Drew Winter on June 3, 1852, and together they had six children.

In 1865, Mary hired William, Sarah's husband, to be her agent and attorney to manage all of the properties the family owned. In return, William and Sarah could live at the Myrtles as their home. In 1867, William was unable to manage the Myrtles causing it to go bankrupt. The property was sold by the U.S. Marshall to New York Warehouse and Security Company in 1868. Sarah Winter, heir to her father, Ruffin Stirling, was able to buy back the Myrtles Plantation in 1870.

According to an issue of Point Coupee Democrat Newspaper, William Winter, while conducting a Sunday school lesson, was called to come outside. As he went to the side gallery of the house, a stranger sitting on his horse, shot Winter, turned and road off. Winter collapsed on the porch and died in 1880, Mary Cobb Stirling passed away. Steven Stirling, one of Ruffin and Mary's children, purchased the Myrtles Plantation in 1880, but sells the property in 1886 to Oran D. Brooks. Brooks in turn sells the plantation to Harrison Milton Williams in 1889.

After Harrison Williams purchased the Myrtles Plantation, he brought his young son and his second wife to their new home in 1891. As the years passed, the Williams family grew, having six more children. The Williams happiness was short lived, when they were hit with tragedy. As the Williams oldest son, Harry, was gathering stray cattle during a storm, he lost his footing and fell into the Mississippi River and drowned. Harrison and his wife, Fannie, were so grief stricken over the loss of their son, they felt they could no longer run the plantation in the manner they felt was needed, so they turned the Myrtles over to their son Surget Minor Williams. The Myrtles Plantation remained in the Williams family until the 1950s. The property was divided among the remaining Williams heirs, and the house was sold to a widow from Oklahoma named Marjorie Munson. It was at this point the ghost stories began innocently. As time went on, these stories took off and became the urban legend of Chloe, the young house slave and the Myrtles Plantation. In the 1970s, the Myrtles went through many owners until James and Frances Kermeen Myers. The Myers purchased the Myrtles Plantation and opened it as a Bed and Breakfast. There are many ghost stories that took place at the Myrtles Plantation, but there is one that has become infamous over time, the urban legend of Chloe, the young house slave.

According to the legend, it begins in 1817 when Sarah Mathlida, the daughter of David (Whisky Dave) Bradford, marries Clark Woodruff. Sarah had already given birth to two girls and was carrying the couple's third child. Woodruff was known for being very promiscuous. Since

Sarah was pregnant, Woodruff began to have an intimate relationship with one of his young slaves. The young girl, whose name was Chloe, was one of the household servants. As time went on, Chloe realized that even though she did not like the sexual demands that Woodruff placed on her, she was in the house working and not outside working in the fields, which was the most brutal work for a slave.

As time went on, Woodruff was beginning to get bored with the young slave. So, he began an intimate relationship with another young house slave. Chloe began to fear the worst, which was being sent to work in the fields. As Chloe was walking past Woodruff's room she stopped to eavesdrop on his private conversation. She began to do this frequently on other private conversations that Woodruff had. She felt that by doing this, she would know if her fears of working the fields would take place. As she was eavesdropping on Woodruffs conversation again, she was caught by Woodruff himself. He wanted to set an example to all of his slaves, so he ordered that one of her ears be cut off. Chloe would wear a green turban on her head in order to hide the scar for the rest of her life.

As the story continues, Chloe was about to do something in hopes of winning her place once again by Woodruff, so she could remain in the house. On the other hand, many have thought what Chloe did was done for no other reason but revenge. Chloe baked a birthday cake for Woodruff's oldest daughter. As she mixed the flour and sugar, she folded in the crushed oleander flowers, which is a very potent poison.

As Woodruff and his family gathered at the table, Chloe cut a slice of cake for each of them. Sarah and the two ate their slice but Woodruff did not want any.

As the day was drawing to a close, Sarah and the two children became very ill. As Chloe was taking care of them, she did not realize she had put a lethal amount of the poison in the cake. Within hours of ingesting the oleander, all three were dead. In a state of panic, Chloe ran to her room. It is unclear if Woodruff sent the other slaves to get her, or if they went to get her out of fear of Woodruff. Nonetheless, the other slaves went to Chloe's room and dragged her out of the house to a tree in the front yard, where she was hung until dead.

Later, Chloe's body was cut down from the tree. Heavy rocks were tied to her lifeless body, and then discarded in the Mississippi River.

Woodruff closed the children's dining room, which is where Sarah, his wife, and the two children had eaten the cake. He never allowed the room to be used again as long as he lived, which was not much longer. As the story continues, Woodruff was murdered. To this day, the children's dining room, where the alleged poisoning took place, has not been used for dining; instead, it is called the game room.

There have been many reports through the years of Chloe being seen throughout the plantation watching over the guests. Chloe has often appeared in photographs taken by many of the guests as well as employees at the Myrtles.

Another urban legend that comes out of the Myrtles is that of William Winter, husband to Sarah Mulford Stirling. According to the legend, Winter was in the house when a man on horseback began to call Winter to come outside. Winter stepped out of the house onto the front porch. The man drew his gun and shot Winter. As the man road off, Winter managed to get back into the house. He staggered to the staircase at the central hallway where he began to climb the stairs. He collapsed and died in the arms of Sarah his wife, on the seventeenth step.

The Myrtles has long been reported by many to be haunted. The urban legend of Chloe cannot be authenticated because there are no records that indicate a slave named Chloe ever existed at the Myrtles. The murder of William Winter did in fact happen but not the way the urban legend is told. Winter was shot on the front porch of the main house by an unknown gunman. But he died outside on the front porch.

If Chloe never existed, then who is the apparition of a young black woman dressed in period clothing and wearing a green turban on her head? No one can find any historical documentation starting in 1796 until present that Chloe, or anyone else close to her description, ever existed. With handprints in mirrors, footsteps on the stairs, mysterious smell, objects disappearing, death caused by poison, gunfire and hangings, one could say for sure that the Myrtles Plantation is one of "America's Most Haunted."

THE URBAN LEGEND OF OLD
SOUTH PITTSBURG HOSPITAL

A large amount of people, if asked, would agree that most old hospitals are haunted. Stands to reason due to the hundreds of people that passed away through the years while in the hospital.

Old South Pittsburg Hospital was built in 1959 by four medical professionals to meet the medical needs of the community. The hospital was constructed on what the locals call the "Foothill" of South Pittsburg Mountain, South Pittsburg, Tennessee. The foundation of the hospital was built on solid limestone rock, and has a natural spring running directly under it. The spring runs into the extreme northwest part of the Tennessee River. The hospital consists of 68,000 square feet, and had a number of additions constructed throughout the years. South Pittsburg Municipal Hospital (SPMH) served the community for thirty-nine years. In 1998, the hospital was closed, and according to the locals, that was around the time the hauntings began.

In April of 1997, Hospital Corporation of America (HCA) moved into the region and held the groundbreaking ceremony for Grandview Medical Center in Jasper, Tennessee. The new hospital had a fifty-bed capacity and was 95,000 square feet. Grandview was built to replace the aging South Pittsburg Hospital.

The town of South Pittsburg was originally called "Pittsburg Landing" during the Civil War. The ferry landing was located about an eighth of a mile from grounds where the hospital was built. Soldiers were transported from the north to the south, so they could make their way to the battlefield of the "Chickamauga." According to the residents of South Pittsburg, their city cemetery has both union and confederate soldiers buried side by side that had lost their lives in battle. Also, within the city cemetery is a small section that was dedicated to the slaves that lived, as well as died here in battle. These graves are marked with unmarked headstones.

In 1778, the Native American Tribe called "Chiaha" lived and worked the land of what is now called South Pittsburg. During the Civil War, the Chiaha Tribe allowed safe passage to the union soldiers to transport and store their artillery. Today, some of the artillery bunkers still exist and are located behind the hospital. The south began to invade the region. In doing so, many union soldiers, along with tribe members of the Chiaha and Cherokee died, and the confederate soldiers emerged victorious when the smoke cleared. The locals believe that this was the beginning of the land being haunted.

At the end of summer in 1862, the union soldiers reclaimed the land successfully, until the end of the Civil War. Although the union soldiers were successful, the residents began to experience many hardships.

This was due to the soldiers taking livestock, foods that were stored, first aid items, and much more. In order for the locals to survive, they realized they could sell minerals, and limestone, which are native to the region. The residents were very successful in selling the minerals and limestone, and were about to experience another opportunity, which was the railway coming to the region. Although things were looking up for the town, the land still had devastating memories of war, death, and destruction. Because of what happened to the people, as well as the land in this region, most of the locals believed the land to be haunted where the hospital now stands.

Through the years, there have been conflicting stories about the hauntings at South Pittsburg Hospital. Some say, the hauntings began when the hospital opened the doors in 1959. Neonatal nurses reported that they could hear babies crying in the nursery, which was very strange, because the nursery would be empty. While others say the hauntings began as soon as the hospital closed down in 1998. But there was one thing everyone could agree on, and that was, South Pittsburg Hospital was, and still is truly one of the most haunted places in the state of Tennessee.

South Pittsburg Hospital through the years has had many paranormal investigations, as well as past employees and visitors sharing their experiences. The South Pittsburg Hospital urban legend is made up of many eyewitness accounts, from individuals to paranormal investigators.

Some employees that worked at the hospital reported many inanimate objects would move on their own. These objects were medicine carts, hospital beds, as well as wheelchairs. Employees of the hospital, patients, and visitors, reported they would hear women screaming. When security would go to investigate the area where the screaming would come from, upon arriving, no one would be there. It was also reported that shadow figures were seen in the corridors and in patients' rooms, disembodied voices were heard when the shadow figures were seen. Through investigating, there is evidence that suggests that young children, as well as adults, remain within the walls of the hospital. Also, there is evidence that two doctors are still within the hospital making rounds and in surgery.

As stated previously, the urban legend of Old South Pittsburg Hospital is made up of several hauntings. The first of many reports is that of a very large shadow figure, believed to be a man. The locals stated that they firmly believe this presence to be that of a pedophile. It was reported by employees, visitors, and paranormal investigators, through many EVP's, and personal experiences, this male presence was extremely evil. In some of the recordings, this evil presence said, "Fuck off!" "Get the hell out!" and "Leave!" He was also recorded telling the other spirits not to talk to anybody. It was also reported that when this presence was near, people would feel heaviness in their chest.

From what employees, visitors, and investigators can tell, there are approximately eight children within the hospital, and six of them stay within the walls of the 3rd floor. According to many of the visitors, there is the presence of a little boy, who they named Buddy, and is believed to be around the age of two. Buddy is the favorite of all employees and visitors that come to the hospital. It has been reported by many that Buddy just wants to play, or he wants to be picked up. Investigators have actually captured Buddy on their thermal video camera. There also are reports of hearing babies crying and women sobbing throughout the entire hospital. According to reports, there is an elderly woman that roams the halls of the 3rd floor. This elderly woman does not like other women, but would call out to men. On the second floor, according to employees and visitors, there are two nurses that walk the halls of the hospital, and often a man that reportedly died from TB or Tuberculosis, being heard calling out "help."

According to employees of the hospital, Hazel is an elderly woman that roams the hospital. She is referred to as the "screaming lady." According to hospital records, Hazel was admitted to the hospital from a local nursing home for mental observation. After three days of her hospital stay, Hazel passed away due to complications from infections. It was reported that when Hazel would scream or yell, you would know without a doubt, it was Hazel. This is due to the rough and gravelly voice she had. Many of the employees and visitors reported that, when they would go down around the area of "Biohazard," they would at times feel or hear someone following close behind them. When they turned around no one was there. In the same area, photos had been taken where an entity appeared in them. The locals named this entity "Hissing Man." It seemed that when anyone got close to his area, he would say "hey."

The basement of the hospital is another area that is said to be active. It was reported that a "fun spirit" remains here. This spirit is referred to as "The Naughty Nurse." On many occasions, she has been asked what her name is, but she never has given her name. The employees of the hospital gave her that name because she has a habit of touching people very gently in very personal places. She has also been reported whispering things or laughing in order to let everyone know she was around. Also, in the basement is a residual doctor that walks around making his rounds. Many have stated, there is a black shadow that is reported to walk right up to you and then disappear. Another entity that has been seen in the basement is an old janitor that passed away in the 60s, when the hospital was still in operation. He has been seen working around the hospital, as well as still looking for his keys.

If asked, many of the locals will say, because of the history and geographical formations, this makes conditions perfect for paranormal activity. One thing is for sure, Old South Pittsburg Hospital has much more within the walls.

THE URBAN LEGEND OF
THE RAWLS HOTEL

Hotels and the south, when mixed together create a very intriguing montage of urban legends. The Rawls Hotel in Enterprise, Alabama, is one of those hotels.

Japheth and Elizabeth Rawls made a name for themselves by developing some of the earliest plants that manufactured turpentine in the county of coffee, in the state of Alabama.

In 1903, the Rawls's wanted to do something that would promote the growth of Enterprise, Alabama. With that in mind, the Rawls's began building a small hotel. The hotel had two stories with the front done stucco. The Rawls's named the hotel McGee Hotel after the manager. But a few years later, the hotel was renamed "The Rawls Hotel." As the building commenced, the Rawls's wanted to create a unique and beautiful hotel. The outside of the hotel was built like that of a Florida Spanish Mission. Inside of the hotel were doors made of rare teak, and the stairway railing was made out of cherry. The fluted pillars, pilasters, window facings, and mezzanine flooring beneath a skylight, were made out of chestnut.

Japheth and Elizabeth ran the hotel for the next few years. In 1925, Japheth Rawls passed away leaving the hotel to his nephew Jesse P. Rawls and Jesse's wife Margaret. In 1928, as the new owners of The Rawls Hotel, Jesse and Margaret began remolding and enlarging the hotel, adding two, three story wings. Jesse and Margaret worked hard to create a very elegant hotel. In doing so, Jesse purchased exquisite chandeliers that hung from the skylight lobby and beautifully carved columns. The floor of the porch was tiled and had three arches. A walkway was also built that went from the porch to between the two newly constructed wings, to the train depot. The Rawls Hotel was extremely impressive to those that traveled by train.

The Rawls Hotel was drawing many visitors to the small town of Enterprise, Alabama, which is just what Jesse and his wife Margaret wanted. The beauty of the hotel was not the only reason for the many visitors. Jesse Rawls was the founder of the first electrical power system in Enterprise. Because of this, the hotel was the only structure to have heated grates and electric lights.

As the years went by, The Rawls Hotel made it through WWI, as well as The Great Depression. It quickly became the place for many social events, meetings for clubs and organizations.

The hotel was making a name for it and putting Enterprise, Alabama, on the map. The Rawls Hotel continued to be the main place for businesses, as well as social functions to gather. This continued until the early 1970s. At this time, the Rawls began to fall in disarray. Hayden Pursley purchased the hotel sometime in the late 1970s, and spent the next three years restoring it. When the restoration was complete, The Rawls Hotel was back in all its beauty and elegance.

In the three years of Hayden Pursley restoring the Rawls, he reported having several very strange experiences. But Hayden had a few stories that he told often. Hayden often spoke of hearing children laughing. While he or his workers were on the 3rd floor, they would hear laughter outside of the bathroom in the restaurant. While Hayden was restoring the Rawls, he knew there were no children present at any time in the hotel. He also reported seeing a girl around the age of twelve running down the halls. But Hayden had one experience that he talked about more than any other.

Hayden was in the ballroom where he was hanging window treatments; when he returned the next morning, he went to the ballroom. As he entered the room, he stopped and looked. All of the window treatments were down, every single one he hung. As Hayden rehung the window treatments once again, he could not figure out how or why they would have come down. This happens to Hayden yet again and on his third attempt to hang the window treatments, a board from out of nowhere flew across the room and hit Hayden. As he stood up, he looked around the room, and just as he thought no one was there. He was the only person at the hotel working that day. As he stood there trying to figure out how he was hit with a flying board, he soon realized that he was dealing with Mr. Rawls himself and Mr. Rawls disapproved of the window treatments he had picked out. It was obvious to Hayden that Mr. Rawls did not want them up.

Through the years, there have been many reports and stories of footsteps being heard throughout the hotel, the sounds of doors being opened and closed, as well as the laughter of children. It was after WWI when the urban legend of The Rawls Hotel was in its infancy. Reports began to surface about strange and unexplained happenings. As some of the locals would tell others about their experiences, they were laughed at and/or ridiculed. The stories that the elderly would tell in regards to the hotel lessened, but the elderly would continue telling their stories among themselves. As the years went by, the stories were passed from generation to generation.

Many visitors, employees and paranormal investigators have experienced interactions with those that still remain at The Rawls Hotel. According to research, orbs, which are free floating circles of light, appear in pictures regardless of the type camera, be it a camera designed for special lighting or the plain Polaroid used for amateur photos. Many have reported smelling tobacco and/or perfume along with temperatures dropping in different rooms throughout the hotel.

In October of 2002, a local reporter, Carole, decided to spend the night at The Rawls Hotel and report on her experiences. The following is an account of her night at The Rawls Hotel.

It was one night in October of 2002; Carole arrived at The Rawls Hotel around 8:00 p.m. After checking in, she went to her room and unpacked the equipment she brought. She checked her Polaroid camera to make sure it was working. Next, she checks her temperature gauge, what she calls her "ghost meter." This gauge is used to check the temperature in a room. According to paranormal investigators, when a spirit or entity enters a room, the temperature will drop.

It was around 10:00 p.m. when Carole set out on her journey, taking with her a fellow employee/friend and a few of the employees from the hotel. The first stop was the wine cellar/basement. According to many reports, the wine cellar was a hotspot for paranormal activity. Children's voices were often reported being heard in the basement/wine cellar. One of the employees that Carole interviewed told her, that he saw Capt. Rawls dressed in overalls working on the pipes in the basement. Once inside the basement, the activity began. Carole's friend stated that she felt the presence of three children, as well as saw them. She described these children as being dressed in period clothing from the 1920s. Carole then pulled out the temperature gauge and recorded a reading of 35°in the basement/wine cellar. Carole then made the comment of it being colder in the basement than it was outside. At that moment, Carole reported feeling the presence of an older man, with salt and pepper hair, a mustache, and a pair of overalls light in color and black shoes. Carole stated that "she could not really see this older man, but somehow she could see him with her mind." She, for some reason, was not frightened, nor did anyone else that was there with her. As the group got ready to leave the basement, Carole felt a calm feeling, as did the others in the group. They all felt as though they were welcome and had an overwhelming feeling of happiness. The group began going up the stairs slowly. They felt as if they were leaving the three children playing with the older man that Carole saw to watch over the children.

Around 10:45 p.m., Carole and her group left the basement/wine cellar and entered the kitchen of The Rawls Hotel. According to some employees of the hotel, they believed that there was a mischievous ghost that resides in the kitchen. Some of the employees that worked in the kitchen reported that, a kitchen instrument would be laid down on the counter, when they would turn back around the instrument would be gone. They also reported that at times you would hear a pan drop, knowing that you had put that pan up.

Carole and her group exited the kitchen and began to walk to the Grand Ballroom around 11:15 p.m. Before Carole went to the ballroom, she interviewed one of the employees. Today, the Grand Ballroom is used for meetings, dining and conferences. But in the 20s the ballroom was used for entertaining the wealthy. Elegant women with their husbands or beau would dance to the music played on the grand piano that was located in one corner of the ballroom. The employee began to tell Carole one of her personal experiences. The employee began telling her story. She went on to say that one night, she was working late when she heard the piano began playing in the ballroom. That night, she knew that she was the only person in the building. She also knew that the piano was not in the ballroom.

As she began her walk to the ballroom, the playing stopped. After listening for a moment she turned and began to walk away, as she did the piano began to play again.

It was now 12:21 a.m., as Carole and her group arrived at the doors to the Grand Ballroom. Carole tried to open the door but was unsuccessful, so she kept trying. Carole said that the door seemed to be very heavy, but for some reason she could not open the door. Finally, after several attempts the door opened to a small hall that led to the ballroom. As Carole entered the hall, she began to feel strange. She thought to herself that her breath became short and she felt a heaviness that surrounded her. Carole reached into her bag for her camera and temperature gauge, but because of the air suffocating her she was unable to find them. She made another attempt to retrieve the camera and temperature gauge from her bag. Carole thought to herself how hard her heart was pounding, as if it were going to pound out of her chest. To top that off she felt she had absolutely no energy. Yet again, Carole was still unable to find her camera and the gauge. This was puzzling because she knew they were in the bag just minutes ago.

The group began entering the room behind Carole. As she turned to look at the others, she noticed her friend seemed to be trying to catch her breath and the color of her face drained leaving her face white.

At 12:40 a.m., Carole and her group sat down to regain their composure. As they were comparing their notes, Carole noticed two of the hotel employees that were part of the group, staring in disbelief. Carole began to talk to one of the employees. She told Carole that what they all just experienced coming through the hallway had happened to several people who entered the ballroom this way. The employee went on to say that she felt we had been selected to be her confirmation of this strange event. She went on telling Carole that she had told a few people about what happened, but it was obvious that they did not believe her so she kept quiet. She went on to tell Carole that she was glad someone that was a news reporter experienced this unexplainable event.

As Carole and her fellow reporter sat to regain their composure, she looked down at her bag. Sitting there in plain view was the temperature gauge and under the gauge was her camera. How could the gauge and camera go from being in her bag, to not in her bag to back in her bag once again? As she sat there looking at her bag that held the items she had been looking for earlier, being a reporter, she had to have had so many questions rolling through her mind, but probably could not figure out one explanation to any of what she had just experienced.

It was now 1:00 a.m., Carole and her fellow employee decided to call it a night. They felt they had had just about as much fun any one person could endure for one night. As Carole and her friend were leaving the hotel, Carole turned and took one last look at this beautifully elegant structure. As she began scanning the hotel, her eyes stopped at the windows to the Grand Ballroom. Her eyes locked on the faint image of what appeared to be a young woman dressed in white. She stopped quickly to get a better look at the young woman. As she looked back at the window, the young woman disappeared just as quickly as she had appeared.

The Rawls Hotel is so rich with history, stories, and her elegant structure brought joy to so many people that came from all over to see her from 1903 until present day. Who knows? Mr. Rawls himself may just greet you at the door and to welcome you in to his beloved hotel.

About the Author

Deborah Lamb is a retired surgical technologist. After she and her husband raised three sons, Deb decided to enter the next chapter in her life which was writing and publishing books. Deb stated she wanted to make her mark in the world by leaving her children and grandchildren a legacy that will continue long after she is gone.